A CHURCH FOR ALL

Gayle E. Pitman

pictures by
Laure Fournier

Albert Whitman & Company
Chicago, Illinois

For my beloved children, Luce and Abel;
my wish is that they will always feel free to be themselves.—LF

Library of Congress Cataloging-in-Publication Data

Names: Pitman, Gayle E., author. | Fournier, Laure, illustrator.
Title: A church for all / Gayle E. Pitman ; pictures by Laure Fournier.
Description: Chicago, Illinois : Albert Whitman & Company, 2018. |
Summary: "Celebrates a diverse community on a Sunday morning at an inclusive
church that welcomes all people regardless of age, class, race, gender identity,
and sexual orientation. Come to the church for all!"—Provided by publisher.
Includes historical facts about Glide Memorial Church in San Francisco.
Identifiers: LCCN 2017040342 | ISBN 9780807511794 (hardback)
Subjects: | CYAC: Stories in rhyme. | Church—Fiction. | Christian life—Fiction. |
Toleration—Fiction. | BISAC: JUVENILE FICTION / Religious / General.
Classification: LCC PZ8.3.P5586836 Chu 2018 | DDC [E]—dc23
LC record available at https://lccn.loc.gov/2017040342

Text copyright © 2018 by Gayle E. Pitman
Pictures copyright © 2018 by Albert Whitman & Company
Pictures by Laure Fournier

Printed in China

10 9 8 7 6 5 4 3 2 1 HH 22 21 20 19 18

Design by Jordan Kost and Ellen Kokontis

For more information about Albert Whitman & Company,
visit our website at www.albertwhitman.com.

Sunday waking

Day is breaking

Let's go to our church for all!

Church bells ringing

Joyful noises

Choir singing

Laughing voices

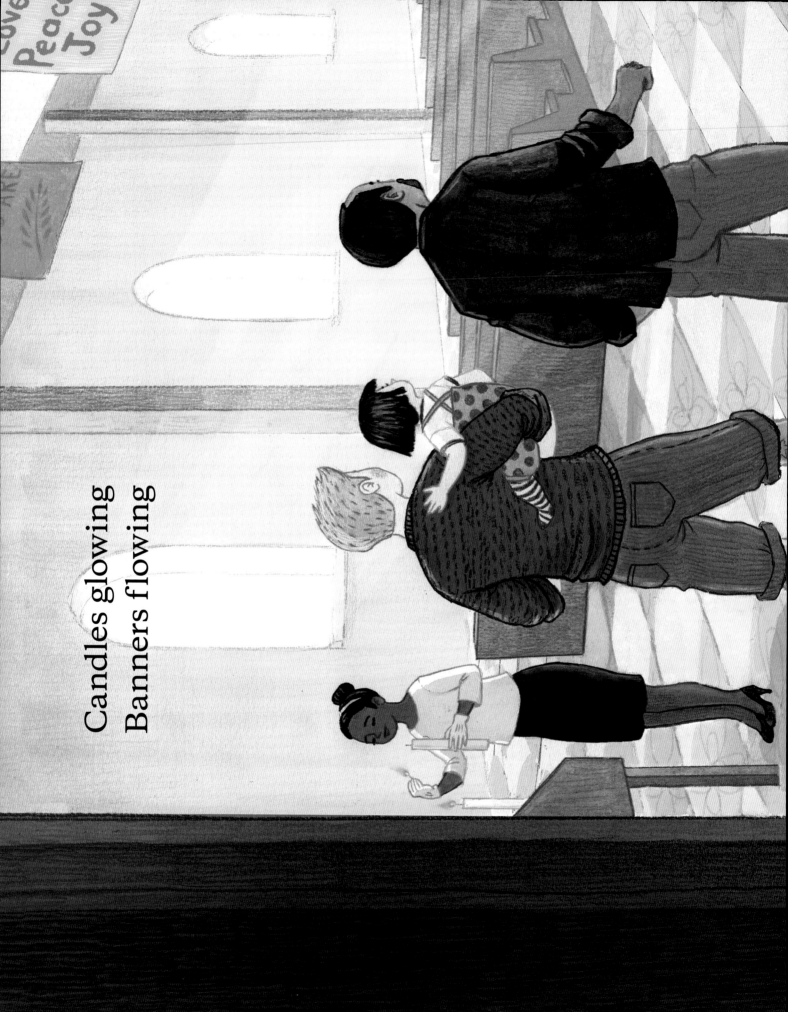

Candles glowing
Banners flowing

Come enter our church for all!

Weak and healthy

Neat and messy

Poor and wealthy

Plain and dressy

All embracing

Spirit gracing

Each one at our church for all!

Bodies wiggling
Mommies reading

Children giggling
Daddies pleading

Toddlers flailing
Babies WAILING

There's room at our church for all!

Hands receiving

Hands connecting

Hearts believing

Hearts accepting

Feel the spirit

Can you hear it?

It's here at our church for all!

Author's Note

Years ago, a friend encouraged me to attend a service at Glide Memorial Church—and I was VERY reluctant. I was raised in a church that wasn't at all accepting of lesbian, gay, bisexual, and transgendered people. Later as an adult in the LGBT community, I'd been to churches where I didn't feel welcomed. Many churches still preach the idea that being lesbian, gay, bisexual, and/or transgender is wrong, and as a result, many LGBT people feel as if there is no place for them in a church. But my friend, who is a lesbian, said Glide was different. "You'll love it," she said. "It's a rock-your-world experience." And it did, in fact, rock my world! For the first time, I had found a spiritual community that fully accepted and embraced LGBT people. That's the feeling I wanted to capture in *A Church for All*.

The story of Glide begins in the 1920s, when Lizzie Glide, a Methodist philanthropist, purchased a plot of land at the intersection of Ellis and Taylor Streets in the Tenderloin district of San Francisco. The construction of Glide Memorial Church was completed two years later. Beginning in the 1950s, many middle-class white families began leaving city neighborhoods like the Tenderloin and moving to the suburbs (a phenomenon known as "white flight"). As a result, the Tenderloin became associated with crime, poverty, homelessness, drugs, and violence. At the same time, a group of new pastors joined Glide, and their values and goals overlapped with the vision of the civil rights movement and other social justice efforts.

Rev. Cecil Williams, who was part of that group, is still at Glide today and continues to be a major presence at the church. By the late 1960s, the pews were filled with people from the most marginalized communities—people who were poor, drug-addicted, homeless, LGBT, and many others.

Since the 1960s, Glide has been internationally known for its commitment to social justice efforts, particularly those that serve the immediate urban community. Glide was the founding site for the Council on Religion and the Homosexual, one of the first organizations to educate religious communities about gay and lesbian issues. Since the 1990s, pastors at Glide have been performing same-sex marriages as an act of social justice. Glide is also famous for its Glide Ensemble, a gospel choir whose music embodies the messages of diversity, radical acceptance, and unconditional love.

Today many churches from a variety of denominations around the country have embraced the same vision of inclusivity as Glide. They are often called Inclusive Churches or Open and Affirming Churches. Many indicate their commitment with banners featuring a rainbow flag or slogans like "All Are Welcome."

The spirit of Glide's mission is what rocked my world years ago. I'm grateful to all the spiritual communities throughout the world, from every denomination, that welcome, accept, embrace, and celebrate us for who we are.

—Gayle E. Pitman, PhD